For those who encourage us to be our truest,
best selves—and for Nathan in particular—M.C.

For my king, Salvador—S.S.

Dial Books for Young Readers

Penguin Young Readers Group

An imprint of Penguin Random House LLC

375 Hudson Street

New York, NY 10014

Printed in China • ISBN 9780525429692 • 10 9 8 7 6 5 4 3 2 1

Design by Lily Malcom • Text set in Fiesole

The illustrations were done in ink, brush, and watercolor, with a bit of Conté.

SMOOT
A REBELLIOUS SHADOW

WRITTEN BY
MICHELLE CUEVAS

ILLUSTRATED BY
SYDNEY SMITH

 DIAL BOOKS FOR YOUNG REA

If life is a book, then Smoot the Shadow
had been reading the same yawn-colored
page for seven and a half years.

And much like two pages in a book, or two ripples in a brook,
Smoot and his boy were inseparable.

Every day they brushed the same teeth, frowned the same frown, and drew the same pictures—always staying perfectly inside the lines.

The boy never laughed.

He never leaped.

And he especially never did anything wild.

So Smoot never did either.

But shadows can dream.
And when they do, the dreams
are filled with color.

Smoot dreamed of singing canary-yellow songs.
He dreamed of doing a dance in wildflower red.

One day, while wishing for sky blue–colored freedom, Smoot heard a *pop*!
He had come unstuck from the boy!

This is my chance! thought Smoot. He packed a few things—some shade, some moonlight, a change of underpants—and hit the road.

Other shadows watched Smoot.
The sight made them brave.
"If he can follow his dreams, we can too."

First, a dandelion's shadow flew away.
The shocked flower watched from the ground.

People who saw the flower's shadow tried to guess what it was.

"It's a baby storm cloud."

"It's smoke from a dollhouse chimney."

"It's a butterfly made of mist."

A cricket and a grasshopper had formed a band,
but were nervous about playing music in public.

Their shadows, however, weren't nervous.
The music they played sounded like cool shade
on a hot afternoon.

A frog that read too many storybooks watched its shadow take the shape of a prince, complete with a cape and crown to croak about.

A dragonfly that longed to breathe fire watched its shadow
become a giant, fearsome dragon.

Even a rock watched its shadow become a cathedral, and then a skyscraper, and finally a castle that reached the clouds.

It was all great fun, but Smoot began to worry that things would get out of hand.
He imagined the shadows of zoo animals uncaged and roaring around town,
or a blue whale's shadow in the sky eclipsing the sun.

But how does one herd wild shadows? A lasso? A net?
Surely they'd slip through like sand.
No, Smoot had a better plan.

First, Smoot built a small castle out of the rock and his friends.

Next he convinced the frog to live
inside it like a prince.

And he told the dragonfly to guard
the gates like a real dragon.

Smoot sang lead vocals with the
grasshopper and cricket so they wouldn't be so shy.
He sang canary-yellow songs. He did a dance colored wildflower red.

Smoot found the dandelion, now turned fluffy white.
He huffed and puffed until the seeds took to the air.

"I'm flyyyyying," sang the flower.

The shadows all decided to return.
Their wishes had come true, after all.

Eventually there was only one person who needed
Smoot's help to rejoin his shadow.

Luckily, it wasn't too hard.
Smoot's boy had been watching all the excitement.
He wanted to be more like his shadow.

So Smoot and the boy laughed and leaped.

Together they acted quite wild.

If life is a book, then Smoot the Shadow's page was now filled with

singing

ringing

flying

vibrant

dancing

color.